ESCAPE TO
SHAKESPEARE'S WORLD

Illustrated by
Good Wives and Warriors

A Colouring-book Adventure

PUFFIN CLASSICS

PUFFIN BOOKS

UK | USA | Canada | Ireland | Australia | India | New Zealand | South Africa

Puffin Books is part of the Penguin Random House group of companies
whose addresses can be found at global.penguinrandomhouse.com.

puffinbooks.com

First published 2016
Illustrations copyright © Good Wives and Warriors, 2016

001

Set in Sabon MT and Bodoni Classic Chancery
Printed in Italy
A CIP catalogue record for this book is available from the British Library

ISBN: 978–0–141–37121–4

All the world's a *stage*,
And all the men and women merely players – *As You Like It*

Two households, both alike in *dignity*

(In fair *Verona*, where we lay our scene) – *Romeo and Juliet*

What's in a name? That which we call a *rose*
By any other name would smell as *sweet*

                       – *Romeo and Juliet*

It was the *nightingale*, and not the *lark*,
That pierced the fearful hollow of thine ear – *Romeo and Juliet*

Heaven is here,
Where *Juliet* lives;
and every cat and dog
And little mouse,
every unworthy thing,
Live here in heaven and
may look on her;
But *Romeo* may not

– *Romeo and Juliet*

Did ever *dragon*
keep so fair a cave?

— *Romeo and Juliet*

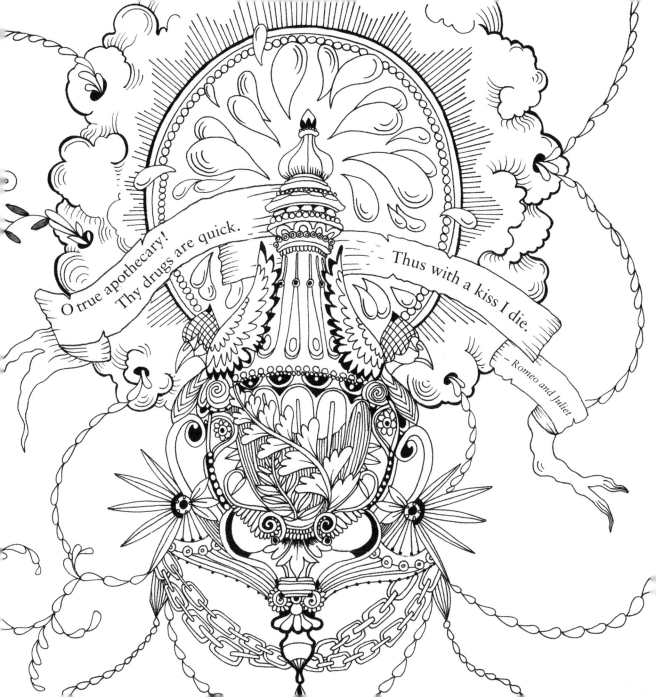

O true apothecary! Thy drugs are quick. Thus with a kiss I die.

– *Romeo and Juliet*

*F*or never was a story of more woe
Than this of *Juliet* and her *Romeo*
– *Romeo and Juliet*

Be not afeard;
the isle is full of noises
– *The Tempest*

O *brave* new *world*,
That has such people in't
– *The Tempest*

My *library* was dukedom large enough – *The Tempest*

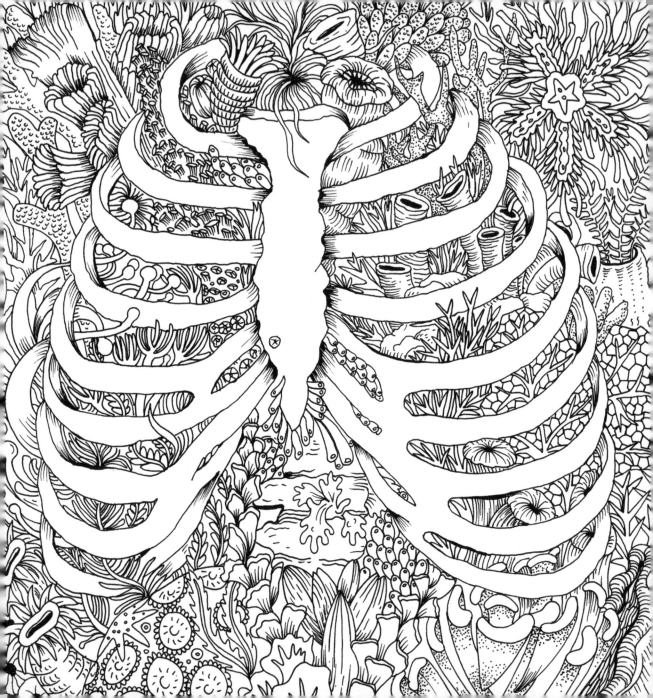

Full fathom five thy father lies;
of his *bones* are *coral* made.
Those are *pearls* that were his eyes.
Nothing of him that doth fade
But doth suffer a *sea-change*
Into something rich and strange.

                      – *The Tempest*

Now I will believe

That there are

unicorns . . .

– The Tempest

Now would I give a *thousand furlongs*
of sea for an *acre* of barren ground

– *The Tempest*

... and you whose pastime
Is to make midnight *mushrooms*
— *The Tempest*

Alas, poor *Yorick*!
I knew him, *Horatio*, a fellow
of infinite jest, of most
excellent fancy

– *Hamlet*

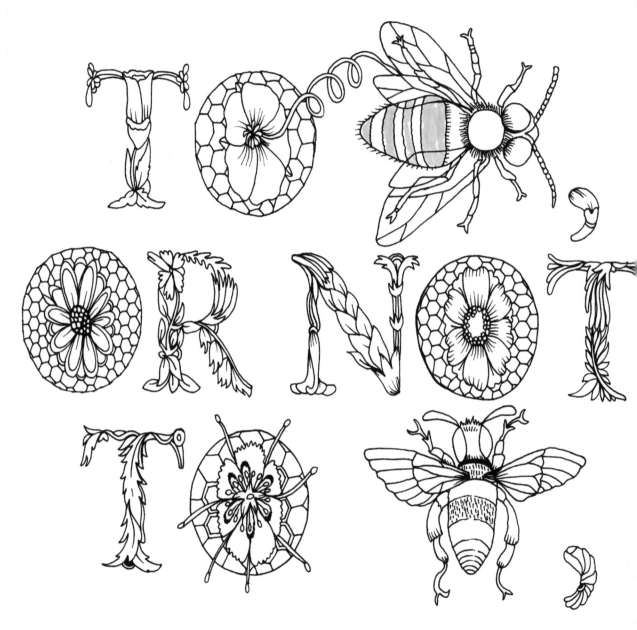

that is the question – Hamlet

Something is rotten
in the state of
Denmark
– *Hamlet*

There with fantastic *garlands*
did she come
Of *crow-flowers, nettles,
ᴅaisies,* and *long purples*
– *Hamlet*

Doubt thou the *stars* are fire;
Doubt that the *sun* doth move;

Doubt *truth* to be a liar;
But never doubt I *love*.

— *Hamlet*

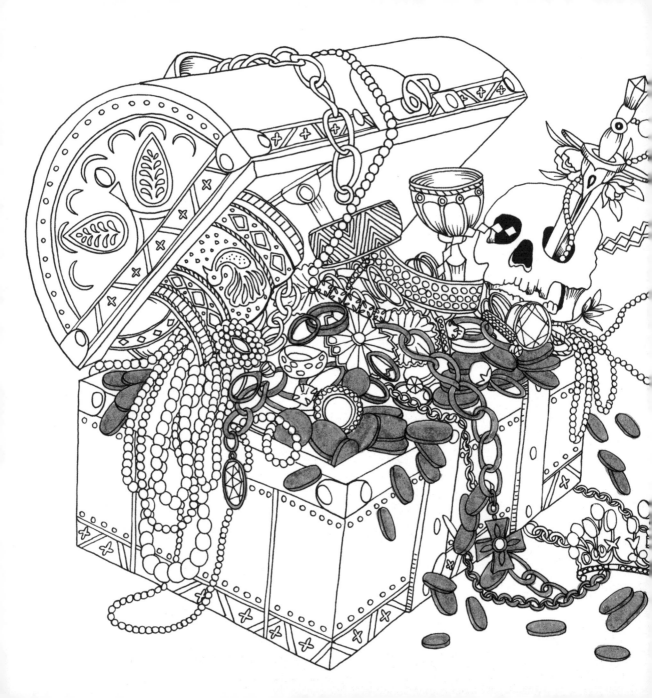

All that *glisters* is not *gold* –
Often have you heard that told

       – *The Merchant* of *Venice*

Your *mind* is tossing on the ocean
– *The Merchant of Venice*

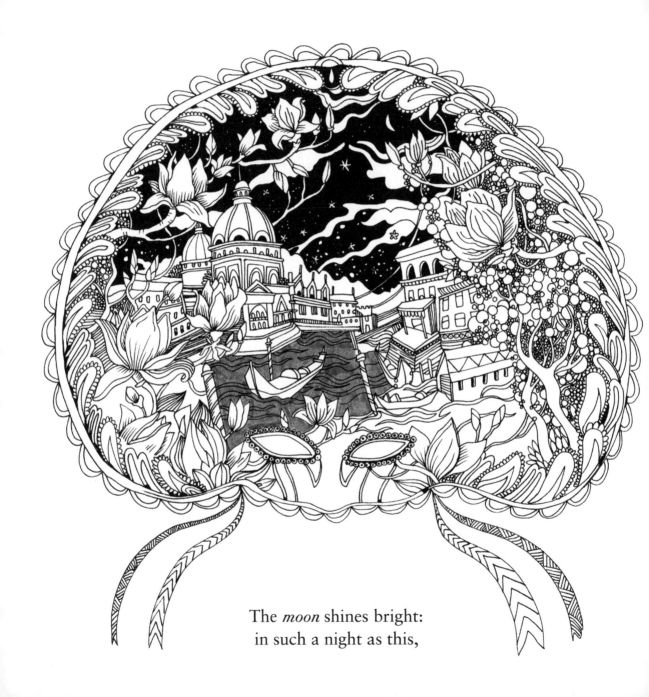

The *moon* shines bright:
in such a night as this,

When the sweet wind
did gently *kiss* the trees
— *The Merchant of Venice*

a Midsummer

Out of this wood do not *desire* to go

Night's Dream

– A Midsummer Night's Dream

I know a bank where
the wild thyme blows,
Where oxlips and the
nodding violet grows,
Quite over-canopied with
luscious woodbine,
With sweet musk-roses
and with eglantine

– A Midsummer Night's Dream

You spotted snakes
with double tongue,
Thorny hedgehogs, be not seen.

Newts and blind-worms,
do no wrong.
Come not near our
fairy queen.

– *A Midsummer
Night's Dream*

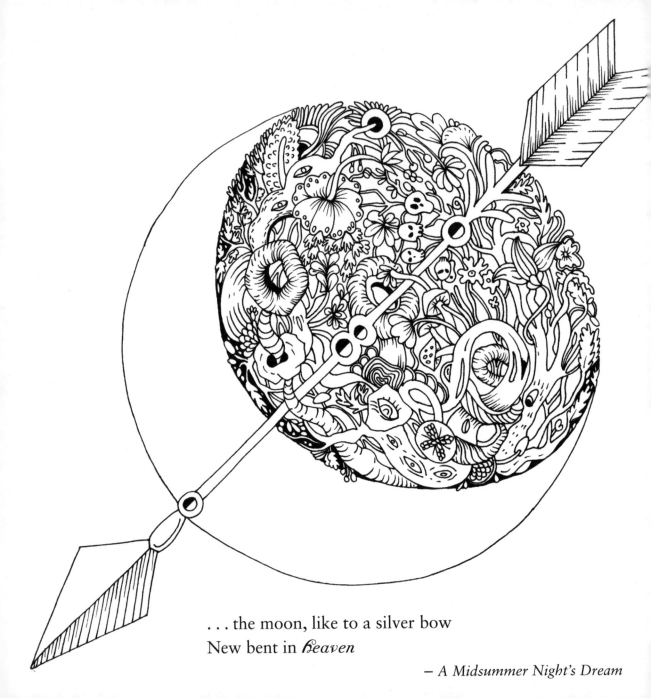

. . . the moon, like to a silver bow
New bent in *heaven*

– *A Midsummer Night's Dream*

To hear the
sea-maid's music
– *A Midsummer Night's Dream*

It shall be called
'*Bottom's Dream*',
because it hath no bottom
        – *A Midsummer Night's Dream*

A *lion* among ladies is a most dreadful thing – *A Midsummer Night's Dream*

Weaving spiders, come not here – *A Midsummer Night's Dream*

Small *cheer* and great welcome
makes a merry *feast*
— *The Comedy of Errors*

No longer from head to foot
than from hip to hip:
She is *spherical*, like a globe.
I could find out *countries* in her
— *The Comedy of Errors*

Stars, hide your fires;
Let not light see my
black and deep *desires*

– Macbeth

Double, double *toil and trouble*,
Fire burn, and *cauldron bubble* . . .

Eye of newt and toe of frog,
Wool of bat and tongue of dog,
Adder's fork and blind-worm's sting,
Lizard's leg and howlet's wing

– *Macbeth*

When shall we three meet again? In thunder, lightning, or in rain?
When the hurly-burly's done, When the battle's lost and won

— Macbeth

Is this a Dagger which I see before me....? — Macbeth

Here's the smell of the blood still.

All the perfumes of *Arabia* will not sweeten this little hand — *Macbeth*

The barge she sat in, like a *burnish'd* throne,
burn'd on the water

– Anthony and Cleopatra

Oh, *excellent!* I love long life better than figs – *Anthony and Cleopatra*

I am dying, Egypt, dying. Only I here importune death awhile,
until of many thousand *kisses* the poor last I lay upon thy lips.
— *Anthony and Cleopatra*

Shall I compare thee to a summer's day?

Thou art more lovely and more temperate:

Rough winds do shake the darling buds of May

– 'Sonnet 18'

True hope is swift, and *flies* with swallow's *wings* – *Richard III*

To gild refined gold, to paint the lily . . .

. . . Is wasteful and ridiculous excess – Richard III

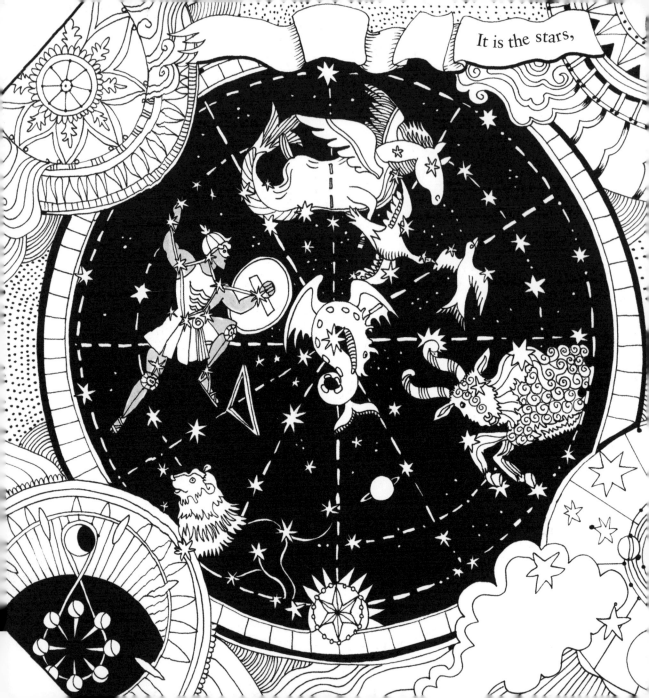

It is the stars,

The stars above us, govern our conditions

— *King Lear*

I am constant as the Northern Star
– *Julius Caesar*

If music be the
food of love,
play on

– *Twelfth Night*

O, for a horse with wings!

– Cymbeline